celadon blue

sky blue

turquoise blue

lavender blue

forget-me-not blue

cerulean blue

duck blue

periwinkle blue

ocean blue

Klein blue

storm blue

Prussian blue

ultramarine blue

Sèvres blue

navy blue

midnight blue

Isabelle Simler studied at the Graduate School of Decorative Arts in Strasbourg. Since then she has written and illustrated several books, all of which focus on the natural world. Isabelle lives in France. Visit her website at www.isabellesimler.com.

for Robinson

First published in the United States in 2017
by Eerdmans Books for Young Readers,
an imprint of Wm. B. Eerdmans Publishing Co.
2140 Oak Industrial Dr. NE
Grand Rapids, Michigan 49505
www.eerdmans.com/youngreaders

Originally published in France in 2015 under the title Heure Bleue
by Éditions courtes et longues, Paris
© Éditions courtes et longues, 2015
Text and illustrations © 2015 Isabelle Simler
English-language translation © 2017 Eerdmans Books for Young Readers

Manufactured at Art et Caractère in Lavur, France.

23 22 21 20 19 18 17   9 8 7 6 5 4 3 2 1

ISBN 978-0-8028-5488-9

A catalog listing is available from the Library of Congress.

The type was set in Oceania.

The Blue Hour

Isabelle Simler

Eerdmans Books for Young Readers

Grand Rapids, Michigan

The day ends.
The night falls.
And in between . . .

there is the **blue hour**.

In that moment, a **blue jay** raises its crest and lets out a piercing cry.

A **blue fox** slips through the arctic cold.

Among the water lilies, **blue poison dart frogs** gather, croaking to each other.

And **blue-feathered songbirds** all sing in one chorus.

The water's surface wriggles with frantic **silver-blue sardines**.

Vulturine guineafowl eagerly flock together, perching on tree branches with a final metallic cry.

The blue hour settles in, and nature becomes still.

The wings of **blue morpho butterflies** sparkle against the morning glories.

Forget-me-nots, **bluebells**, **cornflowers**, and
violets fill the air with their fragrance.

Among the branches, a **blue racer snake** coils itself.

A **bluebird**'s turquoise egg is cracking.

A **Russian Blue cat** vanishes. The countryside is quieting down for the night.

Glass snails stretch their heads toward the sky.

A **bluethroat**, an **indigo bunting**, a **blue crowned pigeon**, and a **red-cheeked cordon-bleu** are silently watching each other.

And at this moment, a **blue dragon** crosses paths
with a **blue-ringed octopus**.

blue monkeys go quiet . . .

and a **blue-tailed damselfly** lands on a **blue milk mushroom**.

They wait for this moment every evening, silently.

and the night softly wraps them in its quiet.